Please email me



# THE SHADOWS OF SAWTOOTH RIDGE

JENNIFER
Bernie McAuley

BERNIE MCAULEY

outskirts press

Shadows of Sawtooth Ridge

v6.0



Outskirts Press, Inc.
http://www.outskirtspress.com

Paperback ISBN: 978-1-9772-3011-9



PRINTED IN THE UNITED STATES OF AMERICA

# Table of Contents

# Prologue

**Relaxing here on** a dead cottonwood stump watching my son and his friend trying to catch that elusive rainbow trout, and gazing at the setting sun over the Eastern slopes of the Rockies. A western meadow lark in the distance, singing his heart out. The frequent odor of the freshly mowed alfalfa hangs in the air. The splashing sound of another trout trying to catch a fly in the creek, as it winds itself down from the high country. The ranch I so loved and left behind to follow other dreams. I had returned to, over a year ago to start a new life.

It was fourteen years ago on a very warm July afternoon, after my grandfathers funeral. I made what I felt would be my last visit to my beloved home. Since it was always thought that my older brother would assumed the management of the ranch for the family. I set out to find my own way in life. The ranch itself bordered the Eastern Front of the Rockies in the "Shadows of Sawtooth Ridge." Resting peacefully between Willow Creek and Willow Creek Reservoir. The following spring I graduated from the university and entered the navy. Beginning a six year commitment as a Naval officer and becoming a carrier pilot. Leaving the navy; I became a pilot for a commercial airline. Marrying a flight attendant, we had two wonderful children (a daughter and son). Every part of my life was on track until I received a registered letter recalling me to active duty.

Flying time between Hanoi and Clark Air Force; 3 hours and 20 minutes. 4 years as a POW and a guess at the Hanoi Hilton North Vietnamese prison. One crew member of the C 141 felt many of our families would be waiting for us there. Down deep I had felt a fear of the unknown and a broken soul. After we left Hanoi a quietness settled over our group.

We've known that the agreement had been signed ending America's part in the war. The last 3 months of prison life had been almost like a 3rd class hotel. Starting in February our prison population began to dwindle. Ours would be the last leaving. There were tears of joy when we became airborne after leaving Hanoi. We all had been through Hell while we were in prison. Communication with our love ones was almost nil. Instead of POWs we were considered criminals and the war powers act of the Geneva Convention was largely ignored by the North Vietnamese until a propaganda film was made. One of the POW's blinked "Torture" in Morse Code while the camera was rolling.

When it finally came my turned; I stepped off the C141 with the Philippine heat beating down on the pavement. A Naval officer escorted Eve's parents and the children over to me. Looking around I asked, "Where is Eve?" Both of her parents walked up and gave me a big hug as her father whispered into my ear. "She passed away just before Christmas." "No!" I screamed at the top of my lungs. Then broke down in tears. My daughter looked up at me and with her bravest voice said. "Mommy told us to tell you daddy, please don't cry." I reached out and we all embraced. Eve was still there and we all knew it.

A few days later another aircraft would be taking us to the United States. The same Naval Officer escorted us out of our quarters to board the aircraft. He would be with us until he thought his duty was no longer needed."Look daddy, it's yours and mommy's airplane." My daughter Jonnie was besides herself. There standing at the top of the stairs where three of Eve's friends and in the cockpit were a couple my friends. Somehow our airline family had managed to pull this off. We were not alone today and we all had the feeling that our journey would not be alone.

So much had changed since returning and assuming my grandparents role as gatekeeper of this special place. I can now look back on it as a new life. It was a time to begin where I left off. I finally came to the realization my first night back to our home in the Twin Cities that Eve was gone, but not forgotten. We all missed her and her positive attitude. The beautiful radiant smile she process for each of us. This story is mine and my family that we began laying the foundation for the day I stepped off that C141 in the Philippines. Eve's memory will live forever in our hearts. She and later her parents took an active role in raising our children while I was absent for 5 years.

# 1

# Returning Home

**It had been** just a few weeks since being discharged from the army hospital. Returning to my grandfather's ranch in Montana, was now a responsibly I had assumed. While in the hospital I convince my family that I could purchase their share. The Naval officer that had been with me and Eve's family was relieved of duty after I had made the decision. Four years in prison and the continuous hazardous duty pay, a wife that made excellent investments, finally giving up my own heritance if the ranch had been sold to anyone else.

It was that decision which had me leaving Minneapolis this morning, and boarding a flight to Great Falls, Montana. Upon landing I surveyed the area around us out the cockpit windows of the 727. The crew older and wiser; invited me into the cockpit prior to takeoff where I occupied the jump seat. A cross wind was making our landing just a little ruff upon arrival. Nothing had changed since I last flew in here as a pilot. Employees knew me and came over to shake my hand or give me a much needed hug.

I entered the passenger terminal and standing there was a familiar face. A man that guided me through my youth and into my teenage years and beyond. Bing was the biggest reason my grandfather stayed with the ranch until he passed away, and he continued to stay with it when my older brother took over. Now I was hoping he was going to hang on when I came along. His age showed with his weathered face and his slower walk. We met each other with a hug in the middle of the terminal where another small crowd congregated around us; mostly reporters from Montana newspapers and televisions.

Since arriving back in the United States it had been one crowd after another. Now I wanted to feel at peace with myself; I figured this was going to be the last since the ranch was miles from any town with a newspaper. Among the small group was a lady that caught my eye. Her face brought back memories of another time. Then of course there were many faces in the last couple of months that all seemed to run together.

She just silently stood there writing my answers to the others on a reporter's tablet. Slowly the crowd dispersed including the lady. A few days later Bing and Laura picked up a Montana paper after a visit to Augusta. All I read was the headline. POW returns home to Montana. I used the newspaper as kindling in building the evening fire. The state of Montana was big, but the population is small. Many times newspapers like to make heroes so they can sell more papers. I was certainly not a hero having been in prison for 4 years.

We drove north out of Great Falls and then north west towards the Eastern Front of the Rockies. It was May and everything was green with the Rockies showing us their best. It was much different than the weather I had experienced the last several years, and unlike the spring weather I just left behind in Minneapolis. I had missed the race riots of the late 60's and a gas shortage that had prices going through the ceiling , Then 2 men walking on the moon. Today we were listening to the radio of some political scandal going on in Washington called "The Watergate" affair. The world and our nation was changing faster than ever before in its history.

I was able to sit in silence and wonder what else I had missed in those years. Deep in thought and just watching the scenery pass. When my family made mention of selling the ranch since my older brother decided on another path with his life. No one else in the family really wanted the responsibility of operating it. I sat in silence listening to them and how everything would work out. They thought I already had a great career so I could keep up with it.

The trouble was that I had no idea if I could return to that life with Eve gone and knowing of the dreams I had been experiencing; afraid of letting anyone know the truth. That night laying there looking up at the ceiling and wondering what life had in store for me now. Somewhere in those thoughts I made the decision to see if I could buy the ranch that I dreamed about all those years in confinement. Maybe it was time to start the process of healing and the ranch seem like the best medicine.

We stopped at the general store in Augusta to buy a few items I might need; since nobody had used the main house for a couple of years. Bing thought it wise to stock up some food supplies before continuing to the ranch. It was mid day and not many customers were in the store: customers that were there came up to me and welcomed me back. Some of them thought a celebration might be in order after I get settled. I paid for the groceries. As we left I started to laugh at a sign hanging on the front of the store. "If we don't have it, You don't need it." My life was beginning to change and it started to come together right in front of that store with a spring snow storm raging around us. I looked at Bing smiling at me as he said, "It's time to go home son."

The ranch's home place sat between Willow Creek and Willow Creek reservoir about 7 miles from town. We eventually came to a "Y" in the road with one leading to the ranch and the other leading onto the "Sawtooth Range." Stretched out along the creek bottoms laid the hay meadows. Today there were cattle grazing in those meadows just outside the main buildings. Bing had fed and checked them for any new born calves earlier this morning, just before coming for me. His wife was standing outside their modular home: waving for us to drive past the main house to theirs. My first home cooked mid day meal was waiting for us and she wasn't going to take no for an answer.

I entered the home and the first thing I noticed, was packed cardboard boxes sitting around on the floor. I looked at them and pointed to the boxes at the same time. " Just wondering if you guys want to tell me something." Well Bing spoke up first. "We did not know who was buying the ranch and we wanted to be ready to move just in case." "When did you find out it was me?" Laura looked at me with a smile. "Last night when you called." It was my turn and I looked at both of them. "When are we planning to unpack those boxes? We have too much work to do around here and unfortunately I hope to be flying again sooner or later. I also have two children I might need help with raising. So don't get any ideas about leaving. A radio with Paul Harvey news could be heard in the background as we sat at the table. I found out later that Bing and Laura had been operating the ranch by themselves the last couple of years. Their son and grandson would come out and help them many times.

# 2

# The Mystery Reporter

**Dakota left the** airport terminal building and then stopped by her office in the Tribune Building to file her story. She would be going home afterwards to her small ranch in the Sun River Valley. She purposely did not asked any questions at the airport. Even though it had only been 9 years since she last saw him; she had kept up with his life along the way. They both competed in high school rodeo and then together in college rodeo. She had always had a crush on him since high school, but he usually ignored her unless they were in a group. When he graduated from college the rodeo team had a party for all the seniors. It was the first time he ever notice me. Then another guy had interrupted us to asked me for a dance and when the dance was done; I looked around and he was gone.

She had heard among some of their mutual friends that he had left the Navy and started a new career in the airline industry. One afternoon while waiting for our parents to arrive on a flight. A airline crew walked through the terminal building and there he was for the first time in years. He recognized us and walked over to say hi holding hands with a flight attendant. He excused himself after we all were introduced; to pick up some paperwork in the airline operations. Her name was Eve and she impressed both Dakota and her sister. Beautiful and outgoing they all conversed a few minutes before he returned with his paperwork. During the time the 3 women were conversing; Eve had led it be known that Larry and her were getting married.

Calling her off/on boyfriend who was an attorney before leaving for home. She mentioned to him her opinion of the afternoon. She had read earlier in a Minneapolis newspaper that Eve had passed away while he was a POW in Vietnam. Leaving 2 children without a mother and a father who most likely needed the time to get his life together. He had mention during the short press conference that he was returning home. Her memory and thoughts race as she drove the 40 miles home that afternoon.

Her memory of the last real conversation with him at the senior party and today when she saw him was different and she could not put her finger on it. She remember him as a proud man, but refused to take credit for his accomplishments. High School and in College it was the team and the students that made up that team. He was at the top of his game in both schools. She remember him saying he had to go elsewhere and create a life of his own because his older brother would assumed the ranch. He had his RCA card, but the Navy and it's flight program offered him a more secure future. She had to reconcile with herself even after one divorce behind her, that she still had a crush on him. When he was in prison she said a special prayer for him to survive and come home every evening prior to retiring. Even though she only met Eve for a short time. DD felt that she was someone very special in many ways and not just a pretty face. That afternoon when they all met at the airport; both of them where carrying fly fishing poles and a cooler was attached to his bag. The sun was setting as she pulled into her driveway with the normal chores to do before dinner was made. It was time to leave the memory and get back to reality.

3

# The Main House

**I LEFT THEIR** home after dinner and proceeded to the main house with my groceries and a duffle bag. My grandparents built this sprawling log home in the middle 50's. It had an extensive floor to ceiling windows overlooking the Willow Creek Reservoir, and the Eastern Front of the Rockies. Standing in the living room area you could look out across the entire property of the home place. The fireplace in the main living area and the master bedroom was formed by field rock taken off the ranch's plowed fields.

Once I entered the home I was looking at decrepit rooms. Even though my old bedroom was left as if it was yesterday I slept there, my single bed and old dresser in the corner was untouched. Model airplanes still hung from the ceiling and a cabinet held trophy buckles and trophies from my many high school and college rodeos days. Except it was in the same shape with dirt, dust, mouse and bird dropping all over the floor including the furniture. Pictures from my accomplishments and the horses that I had ridden through the years hung on the walls covered in dust. No one in the family ever could give me a real answer when I inquired later about why it was left that way.

As Bing and Laura walked through the screen door behind me. A sparrow almost collided with them trying to escape through the same door. Bing shaking his head like he was getting rid of sawdust. When he expressed his feelings, " that there was no way I would bring my family out here until a significant amount of work was done." Logs, forming the walls were starting to turn gray; the dust and just dirt had built up on their surfaces. Floors were starting to bleach from neglect. Mice droppings, dog waste, and even bird droppings had almost destroyed their once polished surfaces.

That evening when dusk finally arrived, I tried to lie down and get some rest. I could hear some little critters running along the walls. It almost felt like I was back in prison again. The darkness brought night mares back that I did not understand, but was told they might be there. Somewhere in the night I got up and walked down to the side of the creek with my sleeping bag. There was some dry wood beside an old fire pit, so I started a fire and tried to relax. Listening to the slow movement of the creek water, night owls, frogs, and the lonely call of the coyotes in the distance I finally found peace. Remembering a Navajo proverb: "Be still, and the earth will speak to you." The storm that was swirling around earlier had subsided.

This was going to become the first of many nights sleeping by the creek. The night air filled with the aroma of the cotton wood trees and burning wood smoothed the soul and mind. Above me the stars that made up the big dipper and Venus were out in all of their splendor. The Northern lights was dancing around the sky as if it was a celebration to the North. Back in my memory I can still remember the many evenings flying across the night time sky or just packing into the back country. Being fascinated by their elegance. Deep in my mind I thought to myself. "Take a rest and feel the deep sleep of a peaceful soul and mind."

# 4

# Getting Busy

**Awaken by the** morning sun and a rainbow trout jumping out of the water for his morning breakfast. I made a call to an old high school classmate of mine who was a contractor. He informed me that he had a friend that enjoyed doing this kind of work and might take the job. We spent an hour on the phone until he let it be known they would be out with his RV the next weekend with his friend.

Getting the home remodeled would take time. It was the middle of calving season and of course we where feeding the cattle twice a day. Fences in the summer pastures needed to be repaired after the winter snows, so we could get the cattle out in a couple weeks. Even the airplane that sat in the run down hangar needed a "Return to Service Inspection and repair." During my time in the hospital. One of the doctors said that keeping the mind and body busy there would be no time for thinking of the past. It looked like that might be the case when I decided to take on the responsibility of this place.

As the days swooped by I was still sleeping by the creek. The contractor working on the house started making progress and it seemed to go faster than any of us thought. It had been a month since I saw my kids that were living with their grandparents and going to school in the Twin Cities. A weekly telephone call and daily letters kept us in touch with each other. A lady reporter called and left a message on my recorder asking if she could come out with her own horse and spend a day. She did not leave me her name, just a phone number. So I returned the call and left a message on her recorder inviting her to come out the following weekend, and help us move cattle to their summer pasture. It was going to be interesting since there would be no time to do what I thought she wanted to do. I never really gave it a second thought.

The sun was just starting to rise over the plateau as we prepared to drive the cattle to the summer range. A man had been hired to watch over them during summer. He would be helping this morning. The lady reporter never returned my call, so I never expected her to make a appearance. It was just prior to breakfast a big fancy pickup pulling a new horse trailer pulled into the yard. The trailer looked liked it had living quarters in the front of it and the pickup was a top of line model. There was a sticker on the rear window that made us all laugh. "Silly boys! Trucks are for girls."

"Man!" I thought to myself this lady travels in style." The country western song. "The Lady in those tight fitting jeans," fit her to a tee as she exited the pickup, opened up her trailer and took her horse out. She then tied the horse along side of the trailer with a hay basket for it to enjoy while she was doing other things. It was the same lady that met me with the other reporters at the airport. All of this time I kept believing it was some other reporter that had called. Laura was standing on their deck summoning us to breakfast and getting a good laugh at her men.

We all followed her into the house and sat down at the table letting her be seated first. All this time she did not say one word. Laura finally asked if I was going to introduce her to the rest of the group. I looked at her for a little help since we had never been introduced. She smiled back at me, "My name is Dakota Dean." Whoa! DD!" The name and the face was finally put together. She and I had competed in high school and college rodeo in our earlier years on the same Montana team. I remember her father had brought calves from my grandfather for many years. The last time we completed together was at the National Intercollegiate Rodeo finals in Denver. It was the senior party held for all the rodeo team senior members that was graduating that year; it was the last time I saw her. I remember trying to carrying on a conversation with her and different guys kept coming over to asked her to dance. Finally she said yes to one of them and the conversation ended.

# 5

# Cattle Drive

**Breakfast completed, we** saddled our horses and made our way out to the pasture were the cattle had been kept through calving season. Beginning the ten mile trek to the summer range. Bing opened the gate and drove a few cattle through it with him. DD, the new wrangler, and I followed him with some 300 head of cows and their new born calves. The process was slow especially with small new born calves.

Looking back it must have been 14-15 years since I last saw DD as we called her then. It was at the college rodeo's party for all the departing senior class. It was my senior year in college and I would be entering the Navy shortly afterwards. I think every college guy at the Denver intercollegiate rodeo was chasing her except me. She wasn't wearing a ring when she showed up this morning and that long and still single just did not add up. Especially with me finishing up college, six years in the Navy, becoming a commercial airline pilot, marrying the love of my life, and having 2 children, and spending 4 years as a POW. Then again I missed more of life in those 4 years then I could ever make up for. I was wishing that I could keep her busy most of the day so I did not have to converse with her. Knowing only too well about reporters that wanted that one story.

It was such a magnificent morning as our little group began to get under way slowly moving up the road for the summer pasture. Our wheat fields on the right and the hay fields on the left. I wondered to myself as we move along about the reason why I left in the first place. Thinking back I believe the family felt that 2 brothers could not get along together on the ranch. So the older one assumed the control of the ranch and it was operated as a family cooperation. Apparently after Eve passed away the family decided that proceeds would stay in the family. This was my ranch and my responsibility now. This time I was not only ready; but thankful that I had the opportunity to come back.

The Eastern Front of the snow capped Rockies stretched out ahead of us. Behind us the bright spring sun was making its appearance rising slowly across the plateau. A cloud of dust made by the cattle was suspended in the air. There was a couple of deer grazing on the rich alfalfa laden fields. Every once in awhile above the noise created by the cattle, I could hear and see an eagle flying above us searching for food. I had a feeling my kids would have enjoyed this day and hopefully would be joining us for the returned trip this fall.

Laura had lunch ready about half way into the trail drive. She had parked her pickup and lunch was being served on the tail gate. DD had worked her way into being part of the crew and we all enjoyed her relating some human interest experiences that she had covered while working for one of the largest newspapers in Montana. Bernhard the gentleman we had hired to watch and live with the cattle for the next several months, was a professor at a university in Spain. His English was broken and he mentioned to us that when he entered the United States to work for me; the immigrations officials did not believe him. I remember the Immigration agent calling me and confirming that what he saying was true. Just prior to hanging up the officer mentioned that, " he wonder why an intelligent person would ever come out to Montana to herd cattle for the summer?" I smiled to myself and said,

"Maybe he just wants to get away from the world for awhile." He had done this work a few times prior for my grandfather and loved the solitude so he could work on research projects without the constant interruptions that he experienced back at the university.

A small RV was hooked up to Laura's pickup that Bernard was going to live in for the next few months. She was going to travel ahead of us to the pasture where corrals and protective cover for the horses and equipment already was in place. A dinner would be ready when we arrived there. The whole day was a lesson in team work and everyone took part. Bing and Laura had taken a horse trailer up a day earlier to our destination, for our return trip.

They say when on a horse you can do a lot of thinking. Some of the thinking was about some of my sleepless nights. The psychologist that spent time with us while in the hospital caution that the down time might be the worse. I had talked to my uncle who was in WWI shortly after I was recalled to the service.

He was in the trenches of France and faced hell and came away from it alive. Unfortunately he had passed away while I was a POW. One evening after I returned to the ranch I made a called to his wife and had a long conversation with her. The conversation led me to asked if he had reoccurring nightmares over the years.

Her answer was a direct "YES" and they continued until he passed away 50 years later. It was so bad that they had spent most of their married life sleeping in separate bedrooms. Otherwise he was one thought full and kind man. He had encouraged her to start painting after many years by purchasing painting supplies. Somehow fishing became a way to find peace within himself after he had tried liquor. They had taken up a homestead like many returning service men did after the war had ended. He was like many young men that came west with the railroad.

# 6

# Catching Up

**The sun was** soaring in the noon sky as we began the final part of our journey. It was beginning to warm up as the day progressed. Some of the cattle where bellowing as we moved forward, making sure their calves where nearby. DD was riding the right flank. She whistled our way, to get our attention shortly after lunch. She pointed to a motion that was in the woods just above her. There was a silver tip Grizzly carefully moving through the trees just following us. Bing saw it about the same time as we did. We all wondered how long he had been tagging along. It seemed odd that it was midday when bears are usually resting with their young or off taking a siesta in some mountain meadow. Now that he/she had been discovered: we were going to keep an eye on each other.

Later I decided to see how our friend was doing up above us in the trees. So I rode up into the heavily tree area where he was last seen. Slowly making my way through the woods: I found no sign that he was with us anymore. There was no tracks where I thought he might have been. So he must have became bored and moved on.

It was spring and the days where longer as we approached the summer pasture gate. Laura had already dropped the RV and hooked it up to the power and water. She had spent the last week or so cleaning it out. The inside really looked like it had a woman's touch with some flowers sitting on the small kitchen table. She even had the horse trailer hooked up and ready for the return trip home.

The evening dinner was all prepared and sitting on the tail gate waiting for us as we entered the pasture. Eating like this just might put on extra pounds that I manage to lose the last 4 years. The meal of sirloin steaks, potatoes, and corn on the cob made our taste buds sit up and take notice. Somebody mention that chuck wagon meals in the old days where never like this. Bing and Laura had been on the ranch for almost 30 years and knew how everything ticked. I was happy that they were staying even though I knew they may wished to cut back because of their age.

We loaded the horses into the trailer and began the journey home. It had been a long day for all of us. Behind us the dust seemed to stretch for miles in the setting sun light. I suggested to DD that she could stay over if she wanted to. The only problem was the house was still far from being done. I was still spending my evenings out by the creek and enjoying it. She looked at me with a smile, "I will be staying, but I have a perfectly good place to sleep." Just before we separated for the night she took me on a tour of her quarters. The horse trailer had living quarters fit for a queen with every item she would ever need. She smile when she mention the old stock trailer I had when I was doing rodeo. I build it in high school shop and manage to keep it together until I entered the Navy. The fact was that old trailer was still sitting over by the barn with no tires on it; rusting away for history sake.

It was a standing joke among our college team about me and that homemade trailer. I was the only member that flew an airplane to school but could not afford a good horse trailer. The team instead of being embarrassed with me showing up at big name rodeos with that trailer; decided my horse and I could hitch a ride with one of them. Even my pickup then was a hand me down from my grandfather. Between the Navy ROTC and a rodeo scholarship my only expense was my food and books.

# 7

# Peaceful Evening

**The sun disappeared** behind the Rockies as I started a fire beside the creek, this had become a nightly ritual for me. I would sit beside the fire and peaceably listen to the sounds of the water as it made its way down from the high country. There was an owl in the distance that played a lonely sound. Even the frogs got into the act as their sound echoed through the night air. An eagle was still flying along the creek searching for that trout that awaken me this morning. Even the crackling of the logs on the fire helped me to forget the past and think about the future. This was my medicine and many times the night mares would stay away. It wasn't long before I heard a rustling among the cotton woods behind me and I turned around to find DD. She stood there with her hair hanging down and totally uninhibited with a smile that lit up the early evening. Privately I always thought she was a beautiful woman. Maybe being shy or I just did not want to be one of the guys that seemed to be hanging around her. I always believed she was above my level.

"Just wondering if you have an extra place on that log?" I just moved over and invited her to sit down. It had been years since I'd really had a conversation with a lady. I just sat there and listened to the night sounds with her sitting beside me. Finally she broke the silence between us, "How long has it been since you've had a conversation with the opposite sex?" "About five years. Where I've been the last several years, there wasn't any women." She smiled and quietly informed me that I did not have to be shy around her. Do you remember introducing me and my sister to Eve at the airport one afternoon? "Some of it was starting to come back now." I answered. " We've ridden together since high school and college. "You treated me as one of the boys for all of those years." "It would be hard tonight to think of you as one of boys." I commented.

We both laughed and the ice was broken. Our conversation lasted late into the evening darkness. Eve came into our conversation and so did DD's only husband and a nasty divorce. "That answered my earlier thoughts while trailing the cattle." He felt that the ranch my parents gave us for our wedding was his. We talked about both of our families. Apparently both of her parents were killed in an automobile accident attending a jack pot roping competition. DD and her sister were quite heartbroken about the accident. Other than the two girls. There was no other children in the family. When it came to my family it was almost past tense. They were not in the Philippines when I arrived and only showed up for about a week when I was in the hospital. Mostly enjoying the spot light and having dinner together each evening. They had an attorney stopped by the hospital with the "Closing papers" for me to sign after I offered to buy the ranch.

Even the coyotes let us know it was getting late when we stood up. I escorted her back to her trailer and I walked back to my peaceful camp on the creek. My sleep was quick in coming for the first time in weeks. No bad dreams that I was supposed to have for the rest of my life: Just listening to the sounds of the night as it peacefully closed in around me.

I was awaken to the crowing of a roaster and a vehicle leaving the yard all at the same time. I dressed and made my way up to the still unlivable house for some breakfast. Attached to the door was a note, "See you for dinner on Saturday night, 7 pm my house, and don't be late." It even had directions on the back on how to get to her house. This was going to be an interesting week for me as I made myself some hot oat meal and toast. While eating breakfast I thought about my last years in high school and college. Until last night she had not made an impression on me, or was it that I was not interested to be in her wolf pack. Life in general the last four years made me appreciate the life I had now.

# 8

# Dinner Out

**It was hard** not to created an impression that I was not anxious for Saturday to arrive . When it finally came I took a look at my clothes to wear and found nothing except a pair of new jeans that I just threw in the suit case when I left Minneapolis and a white shirt from my old pilot's uniform. I had no idea if either would fit. They did although a little loose. The old ranch truck my grandfather had brought just prior to his passing was my chariot for the evening.

It was still daylight when I entered her yard. I got out and took a look around the place. A covered arena was in the center and the ranch house looked like it had seen better years: flowers in the yard were out in full bloom. What came next when I knocked on the door would surprise any guy calling on a lady. A man answered the door and introduced himself as Blake. " I am DD's fiancée." I was about to turn around and leave about as fast as I could, when she called from the kitchen. "I've see you two have met," she said as she entered the living room. "Well don't be shy come in please and I will have dinner ready shortly."

Blake and I were left sitting in the living room making conversation. Apparently he was an attorney in Great Falls and when he heard that DD had invited me over for dinner he wanted to be there to meet me. He called me a "Montana legend." "Not so fast I quickly answered him back. Legends are people that are famous and earned their title." He looked me straight in the eye and said, " You've earned it as far as the people of Montana are concerned." "Haven't you read any of the articles that DD has written about you?" I must admit I've only read the first headlines and used the paper as a fire starter. I've stayed away from newspapers and television: listening only to the radio once in awhile.

Dinner went quite well with a lot of conversation about what was happening around Montana since I left. The conversation was mostly small talk. Blake and DD to a certain extent tried changing the conversation to me several times. I presumed that what I said would be on a front page of some newspaper in a few days. It wasn't long before I was beginning to feel unwelcome. So I got up from the easy chair. Made some lame excuse; and preceeded to leave the house escaping to my pickup. This just wasn't a girl asking a guy over for dinner as I thought and should have known better. It had only been a few months since returning back to the United States. Here I was being grilled by a attorney and a newspaper reporter. I could see the headline in the paper one morning. "Pow spills his entire story."

Going straight home this evening just was not in the cards. Driving through Augusta. I stopped at the Buckhorn Bar on the main drag. There was a poker game in progress in one corner. An old sheep herder sitting on the end bar stool talking to himself. "Pop a Top Again." was playing on the juke box. A few people sat around laughing at some jokes or whatever they were talking among themselves about. After being seated at the bar I just wanted to be by myself. I ordered a beer even though I was not craving alcohol tonight. A lady walked over and sat down on the bar stool next to mine. "Hey cowboy, what is happening?" Without a hint of conversation I paid the bartender and walked out the door leaving her sitting on the stool and a full glass of beer sitting on the bar.

I was driving down the road again when a country western song kept playing on the radio. "Pop a Top Again, I just got time for one more round, "Set Them up my friends, then I'll be gone. Then you can let some other fool sit down." I felt like a fool tonight about as low as a human being can be. Tears fell from my eyes as I remember some more of the song. "Did you ever hear of a clown with tear drops streaming down his face?" Tonight I felt like a foolish teenager as I finally drove into the my driveway. Darkness had finally settled over the bottoms as I made my way to the camp on the creek. It was time to begin my life with my children and try to rekindle my career as a commercial pilot. Haying was a couple of weeks off and it would give me time to train and get to know my family again. I had spent too much time away from them.

Morning came and I sat down to breakfast with Bing and Laura. Just rising over the flat lands of the Rockies, the sun was making its daily presence felt. There was still a fog layer hanging above the hay fields, but the cattle were gone and the stillness of the new day was having an adverse effect on me. A hawk was flying over the bottoms looking for his breakfast. The sound of a meadowlark could again be heard in the distance. You still could smell the manure left behind by the cattle in the home pasture. The chickens were roaming the yard picking fallen seeds from the trees. I was supposed to be happy and satisfied with my life. I missed Eve "My Rock" and her attitude on life. She would of enjoyed remaking this home into her home. Her mother and girlfriends would have been here helping getting things in order.

# 9

# Return to the Airlines

**The Navy finally** released me to fly again after a few in depth interviews with the vet doctor in Helena. I was found physically and mentally fit to fly. It wasn't too much longer the airline invited me to the Twin Cities to begin recurrent training on the 727, since I'd been away for so long. They also indicated that I might want to train on a new aircraft that was just entered into service. It was the 747 and my seniority made me eligible for the right seat if I wanted it. It would mean a longer training period, but the end result would give me International flights and more time at home. While training I could spend more summer time with the kids maybe the possibility of bringing them back to the ranch afterwards. I put my bid in for the 747 with the hope I might get it instead of the 727. The money was almost triple compared to what I was making when I was reactivated so long ago. It took about a week before I heard that I was accepted.

Since I was on leave from the company there had been 2 more employee strikes. The first was the ground personnel, and the second was the pilots. All of them I had missed. It was one of the many conversations on the flight from Minneapolis to Great Falls the last time I had traveled. The crew that met us in the Philippines did not mentioned it the entire 11 hour flight.

While waiting for my assignment from the company. Bing and I had some long discussions about the time I would be away. I came back to manage and run this place and now I was leaving again just like my brother did before me. Bing understood how I felt, but he also knew I had to keep flying so I could pay the bills. It was all going to take time putting all the pieces together. We both agreed that his grandson would enjoy coming out and helping him again do the haying. The harvesting was another matter since it might be ready before the haying was completed. We left it hanging there with a "Wait and see."

My bid for the 747 came through and I needed to return to the Twin Cities for training. Laura offered to help me again, with the children when they finally came to live on the ranch. We all agreed that the house needed to be completed first and that was coming along nicely. It had been a couple of weeks since having dinner with DD and her fiancée . It was an evening I felt betrayed for the first time since returning. Down deep I felt used for the sole purpose of making a person famous in their own little world. There was no way my dreams, thoughts, and feelings were going to be put out there for others to feed off.

I called Sunday evening to Eve's family in Minneapolis and made another call Monday morning to the airline letting them know that I was ready to return to work. When asking about my recurrent and what day I was going to start. They advised me that my bid for the right seat on the whale (747) had also come through. The training for wide body began on Wednesday. There was an evening milk run leaving Great Falls and there was room on it. I called an aircraft company in Great Falls to see if they could update all the maintenance on my plane while I was away. There would be no hurry for it to be done. Everything was coming together as I taxied the plane late in the afternoon into position on the ranch's runway for takeoff.

The small Cessna started down the gravel runway picking up

speed and reaching for the air as it took flight. The Eastern front of the Rockies with the Chinese Wall stretched out on my right as the plane reach for the horizon. Making its way to the final destination. Below me was the Sun River, taking several detours along the way, where it drained into the Missouri River. Today it was just a lazy river adding to the beauty of this place.

Past years it had become a raging lion flooding many farms and towns along its path. Our ranch was built high above the flood plain as my grandfather knew how this lazy river could turn against you anytime. He was always ahead of the game to keep the ranch in the profit side. I smiled to myself as I remembered that he never went beyond the third grade in school. After his parents passed away he made his way out to Montana. His cousins asked him join them raising sheep. Besides only being 9 years old, he was the only person in the sheep camp that knew arithmetic and could read or write . He became the bookkeeper of the cousins business . He worked with them until he was old enough to take out a homestead. Many of his brothers and sisters followed him later from Iowa.

As I made my way to my final destination many thoughts popped in and out of my head. Like the clouds that drifted by me as I flew between and around them. Thoughts about a Saturday evening a couple of weeks ago, the ranch, my children, and missing Eve that was my rock. Even now while flying along; I could feel her presence in the cockpit. There were many times in the last four years I felt that I would never see my family again. Remembering holding both Jonnie and Mark in my arms while in the big rocking chair. Our children were now in the care of Eve's parents. Not only to finish the school year, but so their dad could get his life in order.

Great Falls appeared in the distance as the airport sat above the city. I called the tower for clearance to land. Another familiar voice came on and said, "Welcome home young man. We are glad you could make it." Then he gave me clearance on runway 3/21 with a slight cross wind. You can taxi to Holman Aviation off runway 2/1 after landing.

I answered back, "just wondering if that cross wind would ever cease." He just laughed at the other end.

To my surprise standing there next to the front door of the hangar was DD. Right now she was not the person I wanted to have a conversation with, but there she was. I stopped the engine and set the brake. Exiting the plane I chocked the landing gear, did a quick check of the outside of the plane to be sure everything was in order and signed off on the work order. Since being release from active service; my temper, patience, and conversation were not any of my virtues at this time.

# 10

# WE NEED TO TALK

**SHE WALKED OVER** to me with a frightening look. "We need to talk; can we find somewhere to talk?" "Well, I am not sitting for an interview today. Where is your fiancée to help you grill your headline story?" It was almost 6 PM and my flight left at 10:15 PM. I gave her one disgusting look and knew deep down it was too late to recall my words. Suddenly there was a sign of tears in her eyes, like I just put a spear through her heart. I thought she might walked away, but for some reason she walked to me and fixed her gaze on my face. " I don't deserve that. You and I need to talk before you leave." I did learn one thing about women in my earlier years whether it was my mother or a girlfriend. When a lady tells you; "That we need to talk." You better take the time to talk. She mentioned a park that was close to downtown. We can take my car and go there?" Not a word was said for the next 15 minutes until we arrived at the park. It was a quiet place with a few children playing in their area. Some were feeding the geese that were on the pond. We ended up sitting at a table facing each other. I haven't felt this uncomfortable since my leaving Nam when the guards came looking for someone to harass during the night.

"You stopped at a bar after leaving my home, didn't you." I looked at her strangely, hardly believing what she was asking. "What is the point?" "One of my girlfriends tried talking to you, and you just walk out leaving your beer sitting on the bar and never even acknowledging her. You told me that you never drank alcohol. She mentioned to me that you seemed quite upset about something. I called Laura later and talked with her and she finally said the same thing." "I talked with Blake this morning and I asked him what you two discussed before dinner. I did not hear anything wrong until he mentioned a couple of things that he said. Like introducing himself as my fiancée; and you were making me famous in the newspaper world. Larry he was our attorney when our parents died; he has been around ever since making himself at home. He has never asked me to marry him and if he did. I would say no. I've enjoyed writing about you and maybe "Yes" you are making me and even you somewhat famous. That was never my intention. " I could see the tears building in her blue eyes as she spoke.

I made eye contact with her and in a the most level voice I could. "You must be a good reporter because you went out and did your research and now you want to confirm the story. Yes, I thought I needed a beer that night, but I wasn't looking for company. I wanted to be by myself." Your friend came up to me that night with "Hey cowboy, what is happening?" line."I wasn't looking to end up in bed with some strange woman." "That crowd we ran around with many years ago had every guy in it chasing you including our coach. I had no intention of being one of those. When I arrived that Saturday at your home. I not only felt like one of those guys, but sitting there being grilled by an attorney and a reporter just got under my skin. That is what the guards did while we were in prison. When both of you started to grill me; it was time to leave. Right now I want you and your attorney friend or whatever he is too leave me alone. Let me work on rebuilding my family's life."

"Airline companies these days are obsessed with publicity of any kind that might tarnish their image. I love my job and it gives my family a since of security. Eve had to resign after we were married because they felt a married woman spoils their image. Those women after several years are still trying to get their job back."

Tears started to build again in her beautiful blue eyes as she began to speak. " I never really thought you and I would ever become an item. When we were all together in earlier days, I felt you were more interested in accomplishing your goals than making it with any girl. That day with you, Bing, and Laura, and even Bernhard brought back a life I loved. I've never felt so at home with anyone else until that day. The cattle drive and the evening by the fire, just talking to each other about our futures and our past. I was even able to talk with someone else about my own divorce. Larry, that evening by the fire I felt a connection with you. You're very easy and interesting guy to converse with and you listen. Blake would like to talk about marriage, but with two behind him and paying child support he only used me to make himself look good. He had another attorney in his office that I believe he was having an affair with while we dated. I have no idea why he introduced himself as his fiancée that night. Unless he finally felt threaten."

"Larry I will respect your privacy and stop writing about you. Although I've never met your children; I feel like I've known them through you and I would not want to hurt either of you. I really want you to think about continuing our friendship we formed around the fire that night if possible." Silently I sat there and just looked at her and the tears rolling down her cheeks. "I know I started off on the wrong foot the other night. I did not invite Blake. I let him know that I invited you to dinner and before I knew it; he invited himself. I love your positive outlook on life and your determination to move on, despite your pass. Your in-laws and children sound like the greatest group of people to be in your life right now. The home that you are rebuilding is amazing and I know they will love it. " Your trust in me is not to high right now and I understand that. " Her hands were shaking like a scared animal wondering what was going to happen next.

It took a few minutes before I finally spoke up slowly struggling to find the right words this time. "DD, the right words are hard to defined for me right now. Life has been different for me the last few years. I felt like a fool the other night. Right now it is fragile and I am trying to take it one day at a time. I've lost a wife and four years of my life. There are two children that have felt more sadness in their young lives than most people have seen in a lifetime.

I am not ready for a relationship beyond friends with anyone. Until the other night I was beginning to feel comfortable around you. I'd be lying to you if I said I was not attracted to you. It was comfortable having that conversation around the fire. Trust is something I lack at this time. I have more important things on my mind than chasing women. I have never been that kind of a guy and you should know it by now. Besides every time with the exception of the other night by the fire there is always a guy interrupting us wanting your attention." She looked at me and kind of gave me a smile.

She was trying to smile through the tears. Her hands stretched across the table and just held my hand as tight as possible. She dropped me off at the front door of the terminal. Once again she held my hand before I opened the car door. "Just in case you need help for something , let me know." I smiled and left her there sitting in the car. Thinking to myself a quote from a physiologist mentioned to us one day while in the hospital. "You don't have to see the whole staircase, just take the first step." I walked down to the terminal restaurant were the contractor was waiting . During dinner he mention one little problem that he might encounter. He felt that the kitchen and bedrooms should need a woman's touch. I then thought in the back of mind. Laura might be one person, but she was too busy now to help. The only woman I could think of was Eve's mother Susan that might be able to help even though she lived in the Twin Cities.

"I will see if she can call you and help out."

Flight 40, a 727/100 now, lifted off from Great Falls, Montana right on time at 10:15 PM. It was a milk run to Chicago stopping along the way in a couple of cities including the Twin Cities. 2 AM in the morning we landed at the Minneapolis-St. Paul airport and I caught a cab to my dark and empty home.

# 11

# Lonely Twin City Home

**It felt strange** entering an empty home in Minneapolis for the first time in a couple of months. Going to bed in our king size bed by myself was lonely. So many nights coming home after a late flight and crawling into bed and cozening up to a beautiful lady, was beyond anything I could ever dream. Tonight it was only me in this empty bed. Her memory was all over this home that she was able to make into a sanctuary for her family, away from the busy world. Meal time was family time for all, even when I was out on a trip. Through the few years we were married she had kept many of her airline friends and they gathered here often.

Unlike some airline crew members; we did not meet on a flight. It was a summer of 1966. Our company decided to ground all aircraft until the duration of the mechanic strike. Unemployment was something many of the employees never experience before. She came to a summer employee barbeque party with another pilot. I was there with a few other pilot friends. I managed to sneak some time with her while her date was doing other things. It took a couple of weeks before I got up the nerve to asked her out on a date. The rest of the summer we spent having lake side picnics and just enjoying the Minnesota summer.

We both where on lay off so money was hard to come by. I manage to find work as a pilot for a local charter company. Which meant some great trips to various places. A few of those places were out to Montana close to the National Park system. Many of those times she would go with me if there was an open seat. Along the way she manage to pick up a little bit of experience by flying the aircraft herself. She found a waitress job at a downtown restaurant. When fall came we where both back to work. Later we manage to match our schedules before I finally asked her for her hand.

We kidded each other that just maybe if we got married she might be able to get her pilots license and go to work for an airline. Those days there were no women commercial pilots. Shortly after I returned I found out that was another revelation. Women pilots were starting to enter the field that men only filled earlier.

Seattle was one of our favorite layovers. Dinner or lunch down on the water front and just being tourists and spending layovers browsing downtown shops and having lunch on the water front. A couple times just prior to getting married she would come along on a Montana layover. Both of us would go fly fishing on the Missouri River between Great Falls and Helena. One morning we even ran into a cowboy movie star down on the river fishing like we were doing. It was a beautiful morning as we sat around a pot of coffee conversing with each other. Thinking back she was a master at fly fishing compared to me. We always seemed to have rainbow trout for breakfast the next morning after returning home.

We spent Christmas with her family. One evening her father and I was enjoying a conversation when I asked him if it was alright to asked his daughter for her hand. Christmas Eve night while opening presents, I asked for her hand. Three years later, after 2 children being born our lives was just like any other married couple looking forward to raising children and enjoying each other. Summers at some lake cabin usually with friends up in Northern Minnesota. Winters would be around the Twin Cities enjoying the many festivals that were put on by the locals.

## 12

# Missing in Action

**Then the bottom** fell out after receiving a registered letter the defense department informing me that I would be reactivated in 3 weeks. I had those weeks to get my affairs in order. When I went missing in action, many of those friends were here daily to consul her. According to her mother who finally saw me on television after being captured months later. She didn't even know that I was alive. The Navy personnel that delivered the news only said, "Missing in Action." I could only assumed the emotional pain she had went through before she passed away. I looked back on that day I arrived from Nam landing at Clark not knowing she had passed away. It was a shock for me and if not for my daughter speaking up it might have been worse.

A few hours later I was up and going over to the grandparents home for breakfast and take the kids to school. Their grandparents had kept it a secret that I was coming so it was a surprise when I walked in and sat down for breakfast. I checked into the airline training center after dropping them off at school. They had my training schedule ready for me, leaving me to spend more time with my family. When Jonnie and

Mark found out their dad was going back to school. They were excited that we could actually be together for awhile after so many years. I left shortly after our son Mark was born. He was having a hard time realizing that he really had a father. His grandfather did a fabulous job being the man to look up to during the time I was missing. He was a regular at all little league and soccer games. One year he took up coaching a T-ball team with Mark on the team. Not having their grandparents around after I moved them to the ranch was a worry I had. It would be one more traumatic experience for them.

During dinner, my first evening in Minneapolis we all started to discuss the changes that where going to happen during the summer. It was about time that I put in a request for help from Susan. I related to her the problem about needing a woman's touch in the bedrooms and kitchen the contractor had mentioned to me. She looked at me with a smile and asked. "How many bedrooms do you have in that home of yours." I replied, "Five or six." The look she gave me after I made that statement. "Just wondering if your grandparents ever thought about starting another family." "I was told this was their dream home." I replied back. "Just wondering if Tim and I can spend time with you and kids." She question me. "Oh yes just as long as you can stand all of us being under the same roof." Seriously looking back at both of them. We all laughed and Susan said she would call the contractor after we completed dinner. The problems about moving the children to the ranch without their grandparents all of sudden where solved.

The kids and I was just about to say good night to the grandparents. When Susan walked back in the room and let me know that the problem might be solved. Apparently there was a lady that had done some designed work for the contractor on other homes. He would call her and see if she would be willing to do this one. Then he will call me back in the next couple of days to let me know. It was amazing how problems that came up were solved so quickly.

# 13

# Accidental Meeting

THE KIDS AND I managed to make a trip to Great Falls and the ranch on a weekend away from training. I called ahead to see if my airplane was done and of course it was. Shortly after arriving in Great Falls on one of our milk runs through Montana. Somehow the three of us were able to squeezed into a two place aircraft. It was fun flying again after so long being out of the cockpit. It was even better flying with the kids for the first time. We made a pass over the hay field where Bing and his grandson was working. We learned later that Bernhard the ranch wrangler with the cattle had a bear run in, but somehow convinced the bear to find other hunting grounds. Susan was told that the house would be done in a couple of weeks. It was a day off for the contractor so I thought that we would not interrupt anyone.

All three of us walked up to the house from our landing spot. There was a strange vehicle sitting in the driveway. Just about the time we entered the home. A scream with a bunch of 4 letter words came out of one of the back bedrooms. Jonnie ran towards the scream before I could stop her and entering the bedroom another scream erupted.

Mark and I rushed to the room to find DD on the floor and Jonnie laughing so hard she was crying.

All of us help her up to a standing position. My first question was, "What are you doing here?" She looked at me not to happy with all of us standing there. "I am doing a job for Jon. Your contractor is my cousin. This is not the first house that I've helped him with; I love doing this kind of work." Mean while I am thinking to myself that half of Montana is related to someone. There was a tipped over ladder and a broken mirror on the floor. Glass all over so I sent the kids to find a dust pan and broom.

She looked at me before I could say anything. "You do realize that I would have done this job for nothing if you had asked me. All the guys I know; you have to be the most stubborn bastard, I've ever known." The children entered the bedroom about this time. This was the time to keep my mouth shut and just smile at her, but I did not. "Careful with your language, you are among children. You are amazedly beautiful when you are mad."

I then introduced her to my children and Jonnie just laugh and asked; "My mother used to say those words when she was mad." We all laugh together this time with DD standing there laughing with us.

The training for the 747 was a whole new ballgame for me. It had been awhile since I had to learn a new aircraft. A couple more weeks and several simulator sessions later: I was able to take the right seat on my first flight from Minneapolis to Seattle and return. Two days later I flew to New York and picked up a flight from there to Tokyo and then returned to Seattle, where I would be based. I was still able to build seniority in the pilots group, even though I hadn't flown for over four years. Holding a regular flight schedule in a high seniority base was easier than I thought. I dead headed to Minneapolis for my final exam and hopefully my new uniform.

One of Eve's flight attended friends became a real estate agent after she was married. So with her help the home was put up for sale. My in-laws had already had a few garage sales and most of the furniture was gone. The children and their grandmother decided to keep their bedroom sets at their grandparents. It was beginning to look like we would be driving out to Montana and maybe stopping along the way. Even the children were starting to be excited about the move to the ranch.

Then a problem came up that nobody could solve. Seattle crew scheduling called and let me know that my bid for Seattle had come through. Since I just had been assigned Seattle I was still on reserved so I immediately ended up with the first open schedule. That schedule would be a 10 day trip out of Seattle in 3 days. Changes were in the wind all of a sudden and we now needed to improvise. The house was done on the ranch, but no furniture. Susan made another call to Jon and left a message on his recorder. Back in my mind I now was wondering if DD would somehow be the person getting us into the house. When the kids and I returned from our one day excursion to Montana. All of us filled Susan in on our adventure and meeting DD in the house. So I was not surprised when it was DD that called her back.

She suggested that the children and the grandparents stay in Great Falls for a few days at a local hotel. Then the next day she would take them to the ranch for a viewing of the now completed home. The rest of the stay in Great Falls would be for shopping for house furnishings. "Oh yes, the kids can come along and pick out their bedroom sets, if they wanted to.

Susan informed DD they would call letting her know when they would arrive at least a day out. Her last comment for me with a slight snicker. "Make sure someone has the money so we can pay for this." Susan had the check book and a couple of charge cards. One last comment from her. "When we get done spending his money he might have to do a whole lot more flying just to pay the bills." I did not laugh at the remark. Everything, including her, worried me. All I could do was go along for the ride and keep my feelings to myself.

A couple days later we managed to pile everyone including all the extra luggage into the car. I was deposited at the airport with my bags and they began their adventure to Montana driving. I made my way to my gate. I handed the lady agent, standing at the counter, my pass and mentioned to her that I also could ride in a jump seat. She smiled and said, "Larry we held a first class seat just for you. Enjoy your trip and welcome back." I thanked her and moved on behind the podium to the windows overlooking the ramp, and sat down waiting for the boarding call. These times sitting and watching the crowds was usually a quiet time for me.

Soon after the flight left the gate I noticed that the seat next to me was still vacant. Every seat in the first class section was occupied except the one next to mine. The lead flight attendant in first class brought me a cup of coffee and I asked her if the flight was full. Her and Eve where good friends and she was there when she had passed away. "We just decided that you needed to be by yourself." Someday I just might understand my airline family. They were there with Eve, the children, and her family through it all. The airline made sure Eve's parents and grandchildren made it to the Philippines before I arrived.

# 14

# My First International Flight

**The blue skies** and the Cascade mountains with Mount Rainier in the distance were all out in their glory when we landed in Seattle. Instead of walking into the terminal, I took the exit out of the jet way down beneath the "A" concourse to operations. There I asked an operations agent the best layover hotel to stay. I called the hotel and made reservations. I also made a call to crew schedule to give them a phone number where I could be reached. When I finally settled in for the evening I wondered how far Eve's parents had made it. They had mapped out a route which took in the Black Hills, Tetons and Yellowstone National Parks. It looked like my communication with everyone would have to wait until I returned from my trip. I was really happy now that I took the one weekend to take Jonnie and Mark out to the ranch. Their interaction with DD was amazing since they only met her. I still smiled as Jonnie related to her about her own mother's 4 letter words.

It was back to work the next morning after a small breakfast at the hotel. The four hour call came and I decided to walk across the street to the airport. I entered operations only to find another Montanan flying as captain on my flight. Dick was a World War 2 fighter pilot in the Pacific. I understood that he was awarded the Navy's "Flying Cross" for his heroism on board the aircraft carrier Lexington prior to its' sinking. His own fighter had been disabled from enemy fire while taking off. Among the fighter pilots of that error he was rumored to be one of the best. We both reviewed our flight plan that had been drawn up by dispatch. Since I was the junior pilot Dick suggested that I would fly the first half. He would do the second half.

Dick handled the pushback from the gate. I was on the radio with Seattle operations receiving the load advise. The next chore was calling tower to get permission for a taxi; this plus going through the check list as we taxied to the end of runway. We started for our takeoff and another check list we had to go through. Just as we lifted off Seattle tower turned us over to Seattle Center. Dick look over to me as the landing gear was being pulled up into the belly of the big aircraft. It is yours son for the next few hours. I made a right turn as instructed by ATC out over the Puget Sound and headed North. Our route took us over Vancouver Island, along the coast of Alaska, and out across the Aleutian Islands. There would be a time when there was no communication with anyone. I remember some of the older pilots always would try to bring up ships along this route just to give them somebody to talk to. The auto pilot was turned on just after takeoff, so it was just watching all the instruments. Looking out the window at Vancouver Island as we past gave me a feeling of self satisfaction.

I started out flying my little Cessna 150 to school many years ago and still flying it from the ranch to Great Falls. The aircraft weighted in at 1500 pounds. Up on graduating from college I moved onto the F100 Saber. Weighting in at 20300 pounds, then they added 7040 pounds of armament making an aircraft carrier takeoff fairly hard. Now I am flying a 747/100 weighting in 735000 pounds. It was hard to believe a aircraft so heavy would even leave the ground. When I was reactivated for service over Vietnam this aircraft was only on the drawing boards at Boeing. Now after being away for so long; I am flying it across the Pacific. The aircraft less than 2000 hours flying time on it. The second officer sitting behind us smiled when he mentioned it was just waiting for me to come home. Dick looked over at me with a smile, "How does it feel son." I replied back with a firm statement, "I love it."

This trip would take us to Tokyo, Singapore, return to Tokyo then to Honolulu, San Francisco, nonstop back to Tokyo, and finally returning to Seattle. Some of the crew members that had spent many layovers in these cities became tour leaders to me. Dinner in Tokyo twice, breakfast and dinner in Singapore. A day tour of the city and Sentosa Island brought back memories of my own imprisonment since the English where kept there during World War 2. Honolulu was beautiful. We arrived there just as the sun was rising. When we exited the terminal you could hear thousands of birds singing, it seemed like in one tree. Breakfast on the beach with the crew was interesting. An overnight layover and then returning to Tokyo for our last layover, before returning to Seattle.

If everything worked out right, I would have four weeks off before returning to work. Those ten days seemed to go slowly, but actually it went quite quickly. We returned to Seattle early enough in the morning that I could make the flight to Great Falls. Most summers in the Pacific Northwest the skies are clear with all the Cascades making their presence known to all. Our view from another early morning landing from the Orient and now taking off for Montana was of course Mt. Rainier, Mt. Adams, Mt. St. Helens, and Mt. Hood in Oregon which could be seen in the distance. There was still snow on their peaks and in some shaded valleys around them.

Arriving in Great Falls I was about the last passenger to deplane. Instead of going directly to the terminal, I walked into the freight department behind the ticket counter and operations. "Any chance I could get a ride over to Holman Aviation this morning." I asked. "Give us a few minutes to get this flight out and I will take you over" answered one of the agents as he ran out the door towards an aircraft. Ten minutes later my bags and I were on our way to the small Cessna parked near the aviation company.

# 15

# Returning Home from Work

I DID A pre flight check on my little aircraft and went into the office to file a flight plan and pay the bill. It felt good to be back in my own plane again. I smiled inside myself thinking of going from a 747 with 360 passengers, to a Cessna 150, 2 passenger aircraft. All in one day and less than 6 hours.

My grandfather had purchased this aircraft for the ranch after I finally received my flying licenses. I thought back to that day when I arrived at the ranch from the airport where we had purchased it. He was my first passenger and accompanied me the following day.

You would of thought it was his toy instead of mine. We flew over the Rocky Mountain Front and along the Chinese Wall. We stopped at a forest service strip deep in the "Bob Marshall Wilderness." Somehow he had managed to get some fishing gear in the cargo compartment earlier, so it was a few peaceful hours before returning to the ranch.

The aircraft became my responsibility to make sure it operated as it should. I did a lot of ranch work including watching the cattle up near the mountains. I even did some work detecting forest fires deep in the

Bob Marshall Wilderness. Doing all the ranch and forest service jobs I was able to build up my flight time. I think I was the only student at the university that flew in for school. I smiled at the thought of this so called rich kid with his own airplane. It was not true since I was lucky enough to be there on a rodeo scholarship plus a Navy ROTC Scholarship. I was responsible for all of my other expenses.

My flight took me again northwest along the Eastern Front of the Rockies towards the ranch. It was going to feel good to see the children and find out their reaction after arriving to their new home. Seeing the ranch in the distance I decided to take a fly by, low over the place to announce my coming. It was a welcome sight when it seem everyone came out of nowhere to wave. One more pass to line up with the runway and then land. A slow taxi to the hangar and I was done. Jonnie and Mark came running over to me and each gave me a big bear hug. It felt good being home. Mark and his grandpa helped me push the airplane back into the hangar.

Between the time changes and the long flight times, I was ready for an afternoon nap when we finally entered the house. Tonight sleeping down on the river did not sound like a good idea. I walked into the house and I was amazed what had been accomplished without me. Susan was beaming from ear to ear. She could hardly wait to show me the rest of the house. The last time I saw it was still in the construction stage.

Now it look like a home in some Western Art Magazine. It was my grandparents home and now it would be my family's home. The thought of My grandmother most likely looking down from heaven with a twinkle in her eye. I finally apologized after viewing the work they had done; it was time to get some much needed rest. When I was trying to thank Susan for all she had done she gave me a smile. In her most graceful voice she said, "Without DD's help it would not look like this. She really put her heart and soul into this. Including the Children's bedrooms and the master bedroom." Her husband smiled and looked at me. "Larry my wife did not tell you that we picked out our bedroom also." "Wow! You are planning on moving in too. Shaking my head. "Not quite that bad, but we plan on spending more time out here then our home in Minneapolis. We also would like to buy a place down in Arizona so we can go where it is warm for four or five months a year." "We will be leaving you shortly after the kids start school, if that is alright." I gave it a thumbs up and went to my bedroom.

"Hey dad." I heard a little voice behind me just about the time I reached the door. "That is my bedroom. Yours is over there." Everybody just laughed as I moved towards what used to be my grandparents bedroom. It felt somewhat odd that I was now occupying their space, but here I am. It was beautiful with a large windows looking out to Willow Creek Reservoir and the Rockies. The master bedroom was like non-other, with its king size bed and easy chairs in front of the fireplace. It did have a lady's touch alright. My mind was racing as I drifted off to sleep. Thinking it was still August and it would be four weeks until I had to return to work. Now it was time to be a rancher and help Bing as much as I could. Second cutting was starting and the alfalfa had to be mowed. The wheat was ready for harvesting.

It was late afternoon when I finally awoke from a deep sleep. I could hear two or three women's voices in the kitchen busy gossiping I presumed . Sleepily I walked out into the main part of the house and there was DD, Laura, and Susan laughing up a storm and enjoying each other's company. Dinner was in order and it looked like everyone would be eating here.

## 16

# Summer Ranch Must do List.

**Bing and his** grandson were just coming in from the fields and refueling their equipment for the next day I walked out into the yard with Mark on my heals, and to the building where all of the equipment was kept. Our conversation turned to the wheat harvesting and branding that should be taking place very shortly. We decided that I would spend the short time we had to get the combine ready. Bing and his grandson would continue on with haying. Eve's father was standing there taking in our conversation when I looked at him and asked. "Just wondering if you would like to get away from under the women's feet and help us harvest the wheat?" He looked at me almost surprised and shaking his head "Yes!" It would take most all of August just to finish the second cutting of alfalfa and with some help the wheat harvest could eventually be completed.

There was still much field work to be done but we had to discuss branding. My grandfather always set his branding later thinking it would be easier on the calves. I felt the same way although many of the ranchers did it prior to releasing the cattle out into the summer range.

We all decided to make it the following Sunday which was seven days away.

The evening before branding we drove the cattle into a small pasture near the corrals. Everyone that could ride did and my kids where happy to join us. DD was able to do most of her work from home so she offered to help us also. She had taken the time with the kids and gave them riding lessons while I was gone. My roping skills were still strong even with all of those years that I was away from the ranch. To my surprise DD was pretty good with a rope also. All the way through high school and college I had never seen her rope but her parents used to team rope together in "Jack Pot" competition. Guess she learned from them

Some of my and Eve's friends from the airline and neighbors managed to come out and help. DD and I did the roping and bringing the calves to the irons. Two sets of wrestlers did the branding and various other duties were passed out to all. Laura and Susan had lunch for us at noon. The end result was a large dinner in the evening with a taste of "Rocky Mountain Oysters." Bing and his country western band entertained all of us until late into the evening.

While the band played away DD was enjoying herself with a couple of single pilot friends of mine. One of them came over to me and informed me I better keep her happy or else one of them would be glad to make her happy. I could not believe that I was feeling just a little jealous that she was enjoying herself with a couple other guys. Towards the end of the evening she walked over to me and looked at me with those eyes of hers. "I expect to dance the last dance with you, as usual you are being a hardheaded cowboy." We did dance the last few dances and she made me feel like the only guy in the crowd. My two friends from the airline gave us a thumbs up as we made our way across the floor.

## 17

# Branding and Harvest

**Shortly after finishing** branding we had the combine ready to go. The augur, to put the grain into the storage bins, was set up and ready. Both trucks where serviced and ready. Eve's dad drove one truck with Mark beside him, and DD had volunteer to drive the second one with Jonnie beside her.. DD had been a regular at the dinner since I returned. Susan and Laura handled the house and meals.

Bing and his son left shortly after sun rise in the morning for the hay fields. We had to wait until a little later because of the moisture in the wheat. The warmer sun, later in the morning, would take care of that situation. I climbed into the cockpit of the big turbo machine and drove up the hill onto the plateau. Fifteen minutes later I was in the field harvesting our wheat. It had been a long time since I drove one of these machines. My grandfather always drove the combine and the grandsons drove the trucks during harvest time. Now here I am!

Mark always rode along with his grandpa Tim out to the fields. He then would joined me in the combine cab and would sit on my lap to drive the big machine around the field as it was doing the harvesting.

Tim was able to get some pictures of us together as he drove up along the side to take our load. DD was always just about an hour behind him. She would throw me and Mark up a cold pop when loading. Riding along with DD was my daughter Jonnie. Both of them had hit it off right away after they first met.

August slipped by. The harvesting and haying finally was completed. My next trip to the Orient was leaving in a couple of days. My flight for Seattle was leaving mid afternoon out of Great Falls. Tim and Susan promised to stay until after Labor Day, when I would return. The children had already started school in the middle of August. I'd be gone for about 10 days. I rowed the airplane out of its hangar late in the morning and did a pre flight. I caught myself up on the agenda and loaded my luggage into the aircraft. Tim was the only one that saw me take off and make a right turn for Great Falls where I would catch my flight to Seattle. Just for the fun of it I decided to fly low over DD's home and see if she was there. I saw it in the distance and lowered my altitude to miss the electrical wires. Once over and a "U" turn and over again. She came running out of the house the second time and waved. I tipped my wing and directed my plane towards Great Falls.

# 18

# Finally a Routine

**Three more trips** like this and it would be Thanksgiving. Eve's parents would leave shortly after I returned home and then it was up to me to take care of everything. Laura was a big help in getting the three of us organized. The kids seemed to be settling in and both of them were enjoying the smaller school and making friends. Fall on the Eastern slope of the Rockies can be beautiful. Especially when the cottonwoods start turning. While I was doing chores in the early evening you would hear the geese flying over to the wheat fields on the plateau. An occasional howl of a coyote could be heard in the distance. I was able to spend time with Mark and Jonnie on weekends and after school fly fishing on Willow Creek or just taking our horses out for a short afternoon ride. It was times like this that leaving became harder and harder.

The last weekend of October we gathered cattle and weaned the calves. There were a few semi trailers waiting to transport them to feedlots in Washington. Some of the calves we brought home for replacements in a couple of years. We waited another week before bringing the cattle home to their winter pastures. Up until this time I hadn't seen DD much between trips. The kids seemed to see her more than I did because she came over more when I wasn't home. The cattle drive home was just like the cattle drive up in the spring, with the kids taking part this time. Laura picked up the RV and brought it home first. Then she came back at lunch time with our mid-day meal on the pickup tail gate. She continued back up to the summer pasture and picked up the horse trailer and passed us on her way home. Bernard would be with us a few more days before returning to Spain for his regular job. We all enjoyed his short time left with us prior to returning to teach. Jonnie practiced with her Spanish. Mark's interest was science and that was his field. It was sad when I flew him into Great Falls to catch his flight.

It was early evening when we finished moving the cattle. Everyone, including DD, was there for dinner. I wanted to spend some time with her. Whenever she was here it was with a crowd. I asked if she would like to stay over since we finally had enough bedrooms. To my surprise she said "yes." By 9 PM everyone had retired, leaving just us. Jonnie wanted DD to put her to bed and I put Mark in his bed. The television turned off and quietness had come for the first time all weekend. A fire was in the big rock fireplace and some easy listening music was on. It was a bit chilly in the house since the fall weather was upon us. She gave me that strange look again early in the evening and asked. "Can you remember where you were last year?" "Why do you ask?" I looked at her knowing full well she knew where I was. "You have a couple of kids worried about you and scared something is going to happen." "They can hear you crying during the night and sometimes yelling out."

"I had no idea that was happening." It took two kids to tell me that I had a problem through DD. I would wake up in the middle of night sweating from what I thought was just a night mare. Sometimes I apparently would yell out, to whom I did not know. Apparently the kids became fearful and were concerned for my well being. They feared telling me, so they talked to DD and begged her to talk to me. I thought my life was great until now. I missed Eve and the kids missed their mother. Our lives had changed so much and now somehow I had to take care of myself. "Where do I go from here?" We had some counseling when we transferred from the Philippines to a military hospital in Virginia but I had no idea where to start now.

We talked into the night as the fire continued to burn in the fireplace. I had shied away from any liquor so a cup of hot chocolate was being enjoyed. I have no idea what time we finally called it quits and left for our respective bedrooms. Day light was appearing through the windows when I rolled over to find DD laying beside me. Wow! The last I remember was going to our separate bedrooms and how she ended up here was a surprise. She rolled over with her hair in a mess and no makeup. Those eyes had a way of looking right through you. "You had a bad night last night and scared all of us. Now I know what the children were talking about. So I came in and crawled into bed next to you. Just as soon as I put my arm over you and snuggled up it seemed the nightmare stopped." I rolled over and held her as tight as I could. I knew in my heart what I must do. An hour later I found a card in my wallet with a phone number that was given to me when I was released from the hospital back in March.

# 19

## Unexplained Dreams and Night Mares

I MADE A call to the number knowing of the 3 hour difference between us. They asked me a bunch of questions that meant nothing to me. "We will call you back shortly." I hung the phone up and went over for a cup of coffee. DD took a looked at me. "Don't go too far so I can call you, when they call." I promised her I would stay within her voice. Mark was on my heels as I went out the door to take care of morning chores. He was my son and I wanted the best for him. Life at a young age had been harsh for him and his sister. She was a year older than he and both of them very mature for their age.

DD called out from the house that the phone call came through. I ran up the hill to the house and through the screen door as it slammed behind me, I picked up the phone. I just stood there and answered some more questions about my last 6 months. Unbelievable they wanted me to take my next 10 day trip with the airline; only if I wanted to. They would have transportation waiting for me when I returned. I was to check into American Lake Veterans Hospital near Tacoma hopefully for approximately 20 days. That would put me home just about Thanksgiving.

DD was standing there when I hung up. "Don't worry about us. The kids and I need and love you. Please take care of yourself so we all can be happy." "Love." That was a word I had not heard in years except from my children the last few months. Life from the outside looked great, but from the inside I was hurting and didn't know why. During lunch it was decided that DD would take us all to the airport and see me off. I gathered the group around the table and let everyone know what was happening. The kids came over with a huge hug. My daughter looked at me with the tears swelling up in her eyes. "Thanks dad for getting help. We don't want to lose you too."

The following weekend DD with the kids in tow drove me to the airport in Great Falls. I sat there quietly and began to look back on my experiences the last several years. They were not great memories and ones I thought I could forget. My own family was there when the president met us at the White House. The last evening during dinner. I tried to discuss my last 4 years, but they did not seem interested. I then made the statement that I wanted to purchase the ranch using my share of the ranch if it was sold to someone else. I made the excuse that I did not know if the airline would take me back since there might be mental issues. Before the evening was completed they all agreed they would be glad to accommodate me.

They left for their respective homes the next morning only to send an attorney later with the closing papers on the ranch. Eve's father was there with a check for the rest of the down payment to finish up the process. I now owned a ranch in Montana and I still wasn't released from active duty yet to see what I had purchased. We drove into the front of the airport and gave everyone a hug and a goodbye. Thanksgiving was not far off and I hope I'd be home for it. "The first for both kids and I together."

Ten days flew by like they always did when flying the Orient route. Seattle today, Tokyo tomorrow and overnight, back to Los Angles overnight, returning to Tokyo and another overnight, non-stop to New York overnight, returning to Tokyo and one more overnight, then finally home to Seattle. I was busy the entire time and no time to think about what was going to happen when I returned to Seattle. True to their word a car and driver was waiting for me at the top of the escalator as I exited customs. "Commander I will take your bags for you," as the young seaman took my bags from me and led me to the government car waiting out by the curb. The rest of the crew gave both of us a questioning look. I had managed to take my co-pilot epaulets off thinking that no one else saw me do it. I was back in the military at least for a short time I had hoped.

The drive from the airport seemed like it took forever. It was raining when we landed and did not stop for the entire drive. I drifted off to sleep in the back seat of the car and was awaken in front of the hospital. The driver grab my bags and led me into a waiting room where I was met by a nurse. "Commander we were expecting you. You will be the first pilot from the war that we have in here." Curios I asked her, "Do you mean that pilots don't have problems like mine?" "No by all means no. I understand that most of the pilots that where prisoners of war are being looked after back East. One of the nurses claimed to have seen a few in California." I smiled and looked outside at the rain falling. She also was looking at the same as I was."I can understand this is a little depressing."She commented. She looked at me and asked, "We read that you are the pilot that lost his wife while you were in prison." I am very sorry that your life did not go as plan on arriving home." I looked at her and mentioned. " I have two beautiful children to keep me going so I am not alone." She just smiled.

# 20

# Time to Heal

**The nurse escorted** me to a private room and informed me to take a nap if I wanted too before dinner and our first meeting. Since I'd been up for almost 24 hours it sounded great. My window looked out over the lake with the rain drops falling gently on it. A few ducks where swimming around and they seemed to be enjoying the weather. I laid down on the bed and drifted off to sleep with the sound of the rain and a breeze beating softly against the window. It sent a chill up my back as I went into a dream world or least I thought. This whole scene was really different from the cell that I occupied not too long ago. The only time I saw anyone was when the guards would come to haul me off to the torture room. The meat hook was the favorite instrument of torture at the Hanoi Hilton. A forgotten "I thought" feeling was always present in the back of your mind.

Sometime later another nurse entered the room and awaken me. I was sweating even though the room was chilly from the moist weather outside the window. Taking a shower before going down to dinner was what I needed. I decided to explore a little bit on my way to the cafeteria, finding the workout room, a game room, pool tables, "It's been a longtime since playing that." and finally the cafeteria.

There was a place setting with my name on it among some other men. As we introduced ourselves and finding out that our experiences where very much alike. One of them called it "Post Traumatic Stress Disorder." Many of these veterans exhibited significant psychiatric symptoms. Most ranged from difficulty sleeping because of vivid flashbacks. Others had turned to drugs and alcohol in Vietnam and now at home. Trying to chase the demons away. A few did not experience PTSD until after returning home later. The gentleman that brought this up at the table was a psychologist. I came to realize he would be with us the entire time I was here which was approximately 20 days.

He related to us that he was not only a psychologist, but doing research on the disorder. His research had told him this was something special that the veterans of Vietnam were experiencing. His reasoning behind it was that the veterans of Vietnam came home on airplanes instead of ships like the veterans of earlier wars. Those vets had time to sit down and relate their experiences to fellow war buddies on the month long journey. The Vietnam vets only had hours to relate their stories to each other. Their journey from the jungles of Vietnam in a couple of days to home. Most of the vets he had met had no conversation with their seatmates as they returned. He explained to us that the VA and the government itself tried to sweep this disorder under carpet until just lately. It was a war that many including family and friends detested and did not want to hear the horror of it. Unfortunately PTSD was a delayed stress reaction similar to ours. Many did not experience their symptoms until after they returned home. We all learned that we were here because of a love one, family member, or just a friend beginning to worry about our actions. Suicide was one of those actions taken by some vets. He looked at everyone of us and with a firm belief, "He informed us that we were the lucky ones that someone close to us intervened on our behalf."

He wasn't surprise that I only had a problem sleeping with the continuous night mares I was experiencing. Most of evening was just digesting our experiences in Vietnam and since arriving home. One of them took a long look at me a few hours into the group session. "How do you find time to sleep as busy as you are?" "I really never thought about it in that way." Before I was called up there was always time to spend with the family and doing family things around the Twin Cities, and now I was a single father, owned a ranch and still flying a 10 day flight schedule each month that was keeping me busy the majority of the time. My life did not slow down after I returned home it got busier, unlike some of the others sitting with me.

Among our group there were only 2 POW's. The rest managed to do their time and return home after an unpopular war. Others continued to volunteer for 2 or 3 times before finally leaving the service when the time came. The other POW spent two years in a cage somewhere in the jungles of Vietnam before escaping. His knowledge came from the swamps of the south that helped him to survive the horror of the jungle. Only to have almost being shot by one of his own men.

It was finally my turn to disclose my experiences and feelings. I was shot down on my 6th mission over North Vietnam only to be captured a short time after I parachuted into enemy territory. My entire time was spent in solitary confinement with the exception of the last few months. I had not received letters from any member of my family during the entire time in prison. My biggest worry was that I would just disappear and no one would know any different. That dreadful feeling when my wife would receive the knock at the door. The Naval officer would only say, "Missing in action." The North Vietnamese played on that all of the time letting us know that we were criminals since this was not a declared war.

Shortly after I was returned to American soil I found out that a picture of my capture was broadcast on North Vietnam television and made its way to America. My mother in law saw it on the evening news one night a couple of months later. Once a week I was hauled into the torture chamber for interrogation. The meat hook hanging on the ceiling became the guards means of torture. Most of the prisoners kept in contact with each other through code by tapping on the walls. Boredom, starvation, fear of the unknown, self pity, torture, possibility of execution became a daily routine.

Then I came home to find my wife had died of cancer just before Christmas and 4 months prior to my release. I was now a single father with two children. My own family met us when we arrived at the hospital. It was the 3rd or 4th night at dinner one of them mention that the ranch was being sold and they had a buyer for it. The only problem was that now I was home it could not be sold without my signature since it was a family cooperation. I managed to put them off until the last day when I made them an offer that they all agreed on before they departed the next morning. They acted like they did not want to hear of my experiences. No one asked about my children or Eve's death. My in laws where the ones that step up to help. I think since my father in law had a similar experience after Korea they thought it might just go away. My children had to press the issue that I get help and for that I love them even more.

Day in and day out we spent hours with each other and sometimes answered each other's questions. Many times not leaving the breakfast table in the early morning. The doctor figured; I was one of the lucky ones. Many of the others came home to no job or no one would hire them. A few of them where still carrying a "Dear John" letter with them. Then a few returned to college that was interrupted by Vietnam. Not one came home to a full plate like I did. My slow down period was when night came and I tried sleeping. Purchasing the ranch not only made my life busy, but it was good because I could put the war behind me for much of the day. It was the night when I tried to rest my mind and body that I could not. Sleeping by the creek when I was first at the ranch might have help me sleep, but I will never know.

# 21

# SURPRISE GATHERING

**TOWARDS THE END** of my stay, I was called to the front desk for some visitors. I wasn't expecting anyone since everybody I knew lived in Montana and Minnesota. Standing there waiting for me was DD and the kids. My first question. "What are you doing here? I was coming home shortly?" She gave me a long look and then gave me that wicked smile. "We received a telephone call from your doctor shortly after you check in. He asked if your family could come out and participate in the last few days of your stay. I tried to tell him we were just friends and I was only taking care of the children while you were absent." Your doctor said. "That is great; we will see you then?" "What could I say?"

That evening when dinner was served. It just wasn't my family, but all the families of the vets participating in the program. We all found out as dinner progress what our friends and families were doing here. The doctor informed us that it was their turn to take part in our daily discussion so they could have an insight into our minds and feelings as we theirs.

Explaining not only to us, but now our families about drugs, alcoholism, fits of rage, and even suicide, as ways to escape the disorder. Others manage to get their lives together the best they could even if it had change. Divorce and death happened while they were absent fighting a war that was fast losing its appeal to the U.S. public. Nobody really knew how to have a conversation with a returning family member, or friend. The vets themselves had to learn how to converse with each other. DD looked across to me and gave me one big smile. The psychologist went on to tell us that most of us would be going home in a few days. Others going through another hell of drugs and alcohol would be staying longer. All of us in the group knew who they where and we felt for them. We'd all had become family over the entire time we spent together.

While the children where off doing children things the rest of us spent the next 3 days getting to know each other. DD and I had another problem. The first time I met her is when she came along with her father to the ranch and brought our calves. We did complete with the same high school and college rodeo crowd since we were all from Montana. Until she and I spent that evening on the log last spring. We really where only strangers among a crowd. Along the way she claimed that she had tried to befriend me, but to no avail. It seemed to me that she always had plenty of guys following her and I did not want to be one of them. It was the same as that night when Blake answered the door and informed me that he was DD's fiancé. She gave me a look that could kill most anyone. "He is gone and we haven't seen each other since that night."

One evening during dinner she asked me."Do you mind if I asked the doctor if I could write about this research?" Like she was asking my permission. "You know that you might be mention in the piece if he gives me his permission." "I would prefer not to have my name mentioned." We both smiled at each other.

I tried to explain again my reasoning behind my negative answer. There had been plenty of negative news in the newspapers since I returned. My profession was a commercial pilot and we were held to the highest standards. Alcohol, drugs, or mental disorders where treated as a liability. You carried a lot of responsibility when you where flying an expensive piece of equipment with 360 passengers. One of the biggest reason I do not drink or do drugs. I loved my job and I did not want to screw it up. It gave me and my family the good living we have experience for many years. I had already explain that Eve gave up a job she loved to marry me because a married woman was not accepted in the industry. Many in her group had filed a law suit trying to overturn that industry rule. Like her and many others they were grounded for years before they could work again. I did not need that to happen to me.

Three days flew by and on the last day it was sad to say goodbye to some new friends. Before leaving many of us decided to continue our conversation in letters and phone calls to each other. Somehow DD managed to get the addresses of all of them and even a few phone numbers. Early one morning we loaded the kids in the back seat, bags in the trunk, and us in the front seat of DD's car and set our destination for the ranch approximately 13 hours away. We made it to Missoula, Montana only and found a nice hotel to spend Thanksgiving Eve. The next morning we left early in hope of reaching the ranch by mid day. I'd been gone for too long and feeling sorry for Bing having to do all the work without anytime off.

Yes I was feeling sorry for myself, feeling sorry for the kids having to spend Thanksgiving on the road, feeling sorry for DD not able to spend Thanksgiving with her family. There were two cars sitting in our driveway when we turned into the ranch. Even smoke was coming out of the chimney and lights on in the living room. A November wind and snow storm was beginning to brew when we finally made it the house.

# 22

# THANKSGIVING

**AS WE STEPPED** into the house there was a frequent odor of a turkey in the oven and 3-4 women busy in the kitchen working together. Behind me the children passed us yelling. "Grandma and grandpa!" Eve's father looked at me with a smile and said, "It is about time you got here. We were getting a little worried about you. I took one look at them and mention, " I thought you guys where spending the winter in Arizona." " Bing sitting in my chair smiling and raised a glass of beer to me. "Welcome home son." DD's sister walked up to me and introduced herself with a big hug. She then introduce me to her husband and 2 kids. He was a cowboy from head to toe, walking over and shaking hands with me. I looked over at DD and she gave me a firm. "No I had nothing to do with this." The last 200 miles I sat and drove in silence, upset most of the way home, because this wasn't what I had envision for my first Thanksgiving home would be. It was even better than I had vision for the last 700 miles.

During dinner we decided to open up about our experiences the last couple of weeks. I spoke of the dreams and my children having to intervene by asking DD to talked to me. Because of their fear, I decided to look for help in working it out. DD and children became part of the healing by traveling all the way to Seattle to be with me. I came back from Nam thinking I could restart my life where I left off. The day I stepped off that airplane at Clark and finding out Eve was not going to be there was like being hit in the gut." My own family declined to come at the request of the government. Once again life had changed and I did not know how to get back on the horse. So to speak. It was Eve's parents and Bing and Laura here that had the patience to let me get on with life again. Eve's dad opened up about his time in Korea and his problems after coming home and getting married. Both of them felt I would eventually settle in and keep busy like he did; although Susan claimed he did still had dreams once in awhile. It was my kids that step up to the plate and voiced their concern to DD that something was missing. Talking to the family was like taking a load off of me. John; DD's sisters husband opened up about his life since returning from Nam and his possible PTSD. He was a green Beret and saw the worst of the worst. His wife mentioned that she was at wits end with him and his sad state. All of us felt he could get the help if he asked and he finally figured out he needed help. We all encouraged him to seek it out.

DD then motion to the piano over in the main room. "Why did you have that beautiful grand piano moved out here from Minnesota? Just wondering if Eve was the one that played in the family." Susan looked over at her with a great big smile. "Both Eve and Larry played the piano. There was two of them and we kept the other one in Minnesota. Both of them together used to entertain us with their music." DD smiled at me. "You never mentioned that you played any instrument. It is about time you showed us; don't you think." It took Susan to motion me to play. It had been almost 6 years since the last time.

I sat down at everyone's urging to the piano. Fiddled a little bit trying to get the flow back into fingers and the mind. Then slowly it returned to me the pleasure I used to get playing. The first song I played was "We Give Thanks," then it was onto "Turkey in the Straw," finally "Silent Night." Bing pulled out his guitar, DD's brother in law went to his car and found his trumpet. Everyone joined singing and even dancing together for the rest of the evening.

# 23

# Family Together

**Outside the snow** began falling and the wind started blowing off the Eastern Front of the Rockies. Within an hour most of us figured that nobody was leaving. The horses were in the barn and the cattle in a pasture were sheltered from the storm. We laid out a few extra bales of straw so they would have some bedding. Winter on the Rocky Mountain Front can be a disastrous experience if you are not ready for it. Tonight it was an all out blizzard with the wind and snow blowing vigorously against the windows. We had fires going full blast in the main fireplace and also in the master bedroom fireplace. The new pellet stove in the kitchen was even burning full bore. Tim and Susan at the suggestion of Bing and Laura decided to stay at their home down the hill. DD's sister and her husband would sleep in Tim's and Susan's room. DD would take the master bedroom. I would be assuming the couch in the living room.

I finally had the main room to myself as I stretch out on the comfortable couch with my sleeping bag. "Larry there is no way you are sleeping on that couch tonight. Get your ass in here now." A pillow came flying across the room at me as I ducked to miss it. "You and I are not kids anymore and we are both single adults." She slowly strolled over to the couch in her sexy little pajamas. "I don't know about you, but I am hot for your body." Whoa, not so fast girl. It has been a long time." She gave me a smile that could kill a grizzly bear, "Larry just be quiet and come to bed so we will not wake anyone else."

"Now that might be a challenge." I tried to give her a wicked smile. I put another log or two on the fire, and put another log on the fire in the bedroom. Almost too fast I manage to crawl into bed and she cuddled up to me with her now naked body. All I could think about out loud to the world. "Yes it has to be that girl in those tight fitting jeans!" She laughed. "I must of finally made an impression on you after all of these years. I always thought you were straight and narrow. Maybe I was wrong." I was oblivious to the wind and snow blowing against the log walls and pounding the window panes. The fire in the fireplace burned hotter than I ever remember it. It had been a long time since being with any women. This time it felt different, almost like the world turned upside down. Whatever it was the night seemed warmer and more peaceful than it had for a long time.

# 24

# RETURNING TO NORMAL

**MORNING BROUGHT THE** fragment odor of bacon, eggs, pancakes and hot oat meal in the air. The overnight blizzard had settled down, but was still making its presents felt. Susan and Laura were busy in the kitchen as I slowly climb out of the bed leaving DD there by herself. Sleeping like a baby, only much more grown up and beautiful. Tim and Bing where outside milking the two cows and feeding the calves we had held back from selling. John, DD's brother in law and I decided to feed the cattle out in the hay fields. It took about an hour and the morning chores where done.

Early in the afternoon everyone had cleared out leaving Tim, Susan, and the kids. Bing and I proceeded to feed the cattle for the second time today and lay some more straw bales out for bedding. Tim was still clearing the snow drifts away from the road until it got so dark he had to cease the work. DD also decided to go home, since she had not been home for almost a month. She had a neighbor taking care of the place, but as she put it. "The place needed her tender loving care." Both of the kids and I hated to see her go since she had been a big part of our lives the last few weeks.

Winter had finally set in along the Eastern Front of the Rockies. That old thermometer had dropped below zero and the wind added to the chill factor. Even though I had some dreams overnight, they seemed milder compared to my earlier evenings. Eve's parents decided to stay through Christmas which made my next 10 day trip much easier. I would get up early and make breakfast for the kids before taking them into town for school. A few nights DD would pick them up in the afternoon and bring them home. Friday nights she would stay over for a couple evenings before going home on Sunday.

One weekend Jonnie even went home with her for a sleep over. Apparently DD's niece would come over and it would be girls sleep over. Night life like I and Eve use to have in Minneapolis was non-existent before the kids were born. Even after they came along we always had a date night at least once a week. Now it was some board game or just a good book or me sitting down to the piano and softly playing some music. Tim and Susan did notice that the children grades were improving over their time in public school in the Twin Cities.

# 25

# One More International Trip

**One more Orient** trip just before Christmas was in order. No more flying from the ranch to Great Falls for awhile with the weather so unpredictable this time of year. Just like any morning on the ranch I started breakfast and got the kids up and ready for school. I could see Bing taking care of chores out the large windows. Last night just before going to bed I prepared my flight bags and other items I would take along on my trip. Tim would pick them up later this afternoon after school.

The school was small, but the kids seemed to enjoy it much more than the large school back in the Twin Cities. I heard Jonnie one night bragging to one of her friends back in Minneapolis that there were only 15 students in her class. The boys far outnumber the girls so even though she wasn't interested yet. The girls had their choice of boys. She had her mother's good looks and intelligence. Mark was happy with his teacher and bragged about her at the dinner table. Both of them stayed engaged with all of us sitting around the nightly dinner table. When DD was here Jonnie and her always had something brewing between them.

We left the ranch together in the old pickup that my grandfather brought when I was still in college. The kids loved this old pickup, but sometimes were embarrassed when I dropped them off at the school. It was one of those cold mornings when I finally left them at the school, before proceeding to the airport. Snow still falling along the road and a ground blizzard in progress the drive was a bit slow. Ice had set in overnight so being careful was in order. Arriving at the airport well before the flight left for Seattle I was able to have lunch with the station agents in the back room behind the counter.

The 727 took off from Great Falls making a western turn. I just sat back in the seat and began reading a book I picked up at the airport bookstore. A Spokane, Washington stop and then on to Seattle; the final destination for this one. This mountain trip that began in Chicago and ended in Seattle was one I and Eve enjoyed bidding. Together we enjoyed an evening dinner on the Seattle waterfront.

The rain was falling in Seattle when we arrived. I went out the jet way door down to the ramp. Operations was just below the concourse and that is where I entered the doors to the pilots area. I called crew schedule and gave them a phone number of the hotel I would be staying at. Early to bed tonight and preparing for a flight leaving in the early afternoon tomorrow.

# 26

# Seattle to the Asia

**The 4 hour** call came and again I walked across Old Highway 99 to the airport. Through the terminal, pass the ticket counter, through security, and down to operations. A different captain, and our chief pilot was filling in for the 2nd officer who was in a car accident on the way to the airport. It seemed every senior captain had flown in WW 2 in one capacity or another. This captain had flown cargo flights for the army air force and was quite familiar with the route we were taking today. His service took him into the far east. The chief pilot had flown bombers over Europe in the European theater. He was shot down and spent 2 years as a prisoner of war. Just missing by hours of being executed, because the allied army under General Patton had the prison surrounded before the Germans knew what was happening. These two guys together had more experience than I ever hope too. We all got a kick out them calling me a "Tail Hooker." It had been 5 years since I landed on an aircraft carrier. I had to admit to them that I wonder at times rather I still could do it.

Bob the chief pilot spoke up on our way across the ramp to our aircraft. “I heard that you had a chuffer pick you up the last time. He called you commander, are you back on active duty again?” I gave him a look and said, “No, just an important guy I guess. Some of us where getting together for a reunion.” This time I was taking the 2nd half and the captain was taking the 1st half. The chief pilot jump in and said he would like to spend some time in each seat and all of us nodded our heads in agreement.

I was beginning to love this aircraft as each of us proceed through our part of the check list. It was new and much larger than any I had flown so far. The captain commented as we were watching the passengers board. “When I started flying commercial I could look under this concourse, now I am looking over. It’s time to retire.”

We pushed back from the gate, I started getting all the information about our load from operations. Setting each of the controls as they read me the numbers. We all had our duties as our 10 day trip was beginning. The tower gave us permission to proceed to runway 3/21. It took maybe 10 minutes to taxi to the end of the runway. Slowly we made the turn onto the runway and started our takeoff as the tower handed us off to air traffic control after we were in the air. It was an amazing feeling as the giant aircraft reached for the horizon. I so enjoyed flying most of my life and now I was flying the “Queen. “

Our conversation as we cruised at 35000 feet was casual. We each took a stroll back through the cabin and talked a little bit to passengers and the flight attendants. When I went back there was a movie being shown. Otherwise just the beginning of a 10 day trip for the crew. We all would get to know each other pretty well on our layovers. I did find out on this trip the best way to go shopping was with the flight attendants. So Christmas shopping became a habit when on layovers in Singapore and Seoul, Korea. Tokyo was becoming over price by the early 70’s.

27

# Here Comes Santa Claus

**It was Christmas** Eve morning when we arrived back in Seattle. The airport had been fog in just prior to our arrival. It opened up as we began our approach. My flight home was sitting at the gate and not quite ready for boarding yet. Clearing customs was quick as I made my way over to the gate. Being Christmas the flight was full, but I had authorization to ride the jump seat. I entered the cockpit and showed my ID, stored my bags, and looked at the pilots. "Take me home boys it is Christmas Eve." A lady 2nd officer turn around in her seat and said. "Beg you parted sir." OOPS! The guys in the cockpit smiled at me as we acknowledged that times where changing.

Landing in Great Falls was a welcome sight even if there was a screaming blizzard in progress. Flying over the Rockies the only area that could be seen from the cockpit window was parts of the Chinese wall. Approaching the prairies was almost the same way. I had a feeling it was going to be a challenging drive home after we landed in Great Falls. First was getting my pickup started, since it was so old. I gathered my bags and made my way through the aircraft to the steps in the rear. It was a slow process since the flight was full. Finally to the bottom of the stairs and again I slipped into the open freight door behind the ticket counter. The ticket counter agent was closing out the load and balance paperwork. He almost ran over me on the way out to the waiting flight picking up last minute bags on the way.

A few minutes later the flight had departed, and I walked out the front door past some awaiting passengers at the ticket counter. The sidewalk to the parking lot was icy. Breaking ice on the pickup doors was a challenge before I finally was able to open the driver side door. Getting in the driver seat I put the key in the ignition and turned it. The engine turned over twice and died. While sitting there wondering what I should do next. One of the ticket agents seeing my situation out the terminal front door. Drove a company tug around the building with some jumper cables. 15 minutes later I was on the road home. Thanking the agent for his help and wishing him a "Merry Christmas."

It had been a long time since driving in this weather. Icy roads and snow piled up on each side of the road from the snow plow that most likely went through earlier. Even if the pickup was outdated it managed to travel through the snow quite well. Traveling through Augusta all the stores and even the one gas station was closed. Thinking to myself since it was Christmas Eve. I was glad to have done my Christmas shopping during my last layover as most of the crew did.

I made it to the where the roads split one leading West and the other going to the ranch. My old trustworthy truck decided it wasn't going any farer. Lucky for me I had left a heavy winter coat in the seat and barn boots on the passenger side floor. Through the years my parents and grandparents taught me well about Montana winter weather. It was about a quarter of mile to the house and I loaded all the presents in a gunny sack and proceeded down the road to the ranch. "Here comes Santa Claus!"

# 28

# Tis the Season

**Our first winter** on the Eastern Slopes of the Rockies. My whole family was finding out just how harsh it could be. This was going to be our first Christmas together in years that both kids could remember. There were so many times in the last several years; I believed that I would never spend Christmas or even see my family again here on earth. Someone finally saw me coming down the road from the front room windows.

What a reception when I finally made my way to the door. "Daddy, Daddy, Daddy; you made it home. Grandma and grandpa thought you might not." I looked over at Susan and she shook her head in agreement with her granddaughter. Despite all the road blocks with the Montana's unpredictable weather I wasn't going to miss my first real Christmas at home in years.

Tim and I decided to give Bing a break so him and Laura could visit with their children and grandchildren. We both went out to feed the cattle and roll some more straw bales out for bedding. Straw had become a stable this winter account of the weather. Tim became a great hand to have around these days. Once he learned how to milk cows, there was no way anyone else was going to do it while he was here. It was fun watching him milking and squirting the cats around him begging for his attention. Susan was always busy doing something around the house. Her and Laura always join to make the noon day meal and she always prepared the school lunches for the next day. Now that the children were on Christmas breaks it was one chore that did not need attending to.

Tim and Susan had finally made their home in Arizona and flew to Montana just before Thanksgiving. DD and Susan worked on making the dinner together. DD who had arrived a day early at the urging of the kids and their grandparents. Spent most of the morning in the master bedroom wrapping presents for everyone. Her sister and family also arrived on Christmas Eve earlier having to walk the last quarter of mile from the main road just like I did. I made sure that DD's and all the adults where already wrapped and under the tree. There was always a tradition in Eve's family that one present would be opened on Christmas Eve. It certainly wasn't going to change this year.

We sat down to dinner and Susan led the group in a prayer. All of us was surprise when DD spoke up at the conclusion. "Lets us say a prayer in remembrance of the one person that is here in spirit with us tonight, Eve." Jonnie recited the prayer she had written with DD's help. When she concluded there wasn't a dry eye at the table. Jonnie wanted to remember her mother tonight. Eve's parents after all that had happen to them the past couple of years. Losing their only daughter and becoming guardians for two grandchildren with no hope of a father ever returning to the picture. That night around the Christmas Eve table there was more love than many of us had in years.

Dinner completed and everyone sitting around the tree ready to open that one present. Life on the ranch was much different than in the Twin Cities. Tonight it was a board game or just conversation between everyone including the children. Since I began playing the piano again; it had become a evening tradition with Bing, Laura, and DD's brother in law joining in with me to provide nightly entertainment when I was home. Every one stayed up a little bit later tonight to watch mid-night mass. This was a first for me since I had never been to mid night service in my whole life. There were many nights while in prison I would look up to heaven and pray; always wondering if he was still there listening.

Christmas morning brought everyone back into the front room mostly in their pajamas. DD was up just a bit earlier and made her way to each of the children's bedrooms. Like a kid herself, she awaken each child with a little whisper. "Santa was here. You better check it out." Both Jonnie and Mark came screaming out of their bedrooms. Sleeping in was out of the question after that.

Tim, John, and I went out into the well below zero weather to feed the livestock and milk the cows. It took a bit longer than usual. As four impatient children waited anxiously for us to get done. Breakfast was ready when we returned to house and all the excitement still going on. Presents around the tree where still there unopened. DD went over and picked each one up after breakfast and handed them to Tim, Susan, and myself. I went over to the tree and picked hers up and handed it to her. DD's sister found their presents also under the tree and she handed each one out to her family.

Susan and Tim open both of theirs first. It was an oil painting of myself in a Navy uniform, Eve with our two children taken just before I left for Vietnam. DD had found a photo among Jonnies belongings while unpacking them last summer. She had painted it herself. I held my breath as I could see tears in both of their eyes. Then it was the children's time to open theirs. I opened mine from DD bringing back some of the great memories. It was a photo that DD had made into an oil painting of her and I years ago at the National Intercollegiate rodeo. One I never even knew existed. She holding her buckle and I holding my buckle. The entire college team was standing around the National Trophy we had won. I took a look at her as she was smiling. "Love you cowboy." Looking up I realize everyone was looking at me and I was sitting there dumb founded.

Jonnie seeing that DD was still holding her present insisting that it was her turn now. She opened one and inside was another one. Inside that one there was one more small one. She pulled out a note in the last one. It read, "Look over at Larry, Mark, and Jonnie." We were sitting there together holding a small velvet case opened up and a wedding ring on displayed. "Any chance you would like to be a part of this family?" I tried to asked in a very nervous voice. She looked at Susan, Tim, Jonnie, Mark, and me with one big smile that made the morning light up. Her only question, "are you guys really sure you want me?" Everyone chimed in. "Yes!"

# 29

# A New Year

**The winter snows** melted away and in the distance you could hear the Western meadowlark singing its familiar song. I spent 4 years dreaming of the beauty of the Rocky Mountain Front. They never disappointed me with their sunsets each evening. There was still snow on those peaks in June and sometimes the late afternoon breezes where chilly yet. The cattle had been moved to their summer pasture after all of their calves had been born. Wheat had been planted in the fields on the plateau and the alfalfa was starting to grow in the river bottoms. My 10 day trips to the Orient happen just about every four weeks. Sometimes they where more and sometimes less than 10 day.

The ladies are in Great Falls this afternoon leaving Mark with his friend here trying to catch that elusive trout. It has been over a year since I made that journey from Hanoi to Clark Air Force Base in the Philippines. My children are a year older and growing faster each day. Everyone including DD realizes that there was something very special between Eve and I. They all know that no one can replace her. The kids are loving it that DD will become their step mother. Jonnie sometimes calls her mother. She keeps finding little notes in the children's hidden treasures that Eve planted before she passed away. When I finally started opening up my things that came with the moving van from the Twin Cities; I also found little notes left for me. There was one note in there also to be open by the person that I would marry if it came to that. DD just happen to be in the kitchen making dinner. I slowly walked in and gave her the envelope. We both read it together and about that time both children walked into the room. Yes there were tears in both of our eyes.

Saint Matthias Mission Church in Augusta was deck out for the wedding on a beautiful Saturday afternoon in June. All the years that DD and I hung out with the same group. I had never seen her in a dress until that day. Tim, Eve's father would do the honor of giving DD away. John, DD's brother in law was my best man. Susan and DD's sister were the bridesmaids, Jonnie was the flower girl and Mark the ring bearer. Since I was reassigned to a Naval reserve unit, I wore my "Dress Whites." I was proud of all of my ribbons I had earned along the way. When DD met me at the altar she in a low whisper, "Wow! I gave up a cowboy to marry a war hero. Hope you can handle me." Bing's country band with Laura as their singer played for the reception.

Members of my own family even came to meet the lady I was marrying. Many of the bad vibes I felt when I returned home and decided to purchase the ranch had disappeared. Most of them loved the ranch house that had been completely renovated before bringing my family out from Minneapolis. DD's and Susan's marks where seen everywhere in the home. These two became like mother and daughter in the last several months. Both of them took on the wedding planning together and made a success of it.

The wedding party retired to the ranch with the band and most of the guests. It was nearing dusk as we decided to leave for a honeymoon. Moving the airplane out of its hangar. Our bags where already loaded as we climbed in and taxied to the gravel runway. This would be DDs first flight with the hope of many others.

The little Cessna slowly started reaching for the blue sky. Higher and higher it climbed making a left turn over the ranch as we could see the ones left behind waving. The sun was beginning to set over the Rocky Mountain Front with their snowcapped peaks. Towards Great Falls to begin our journey of life. She looked over at me and put her hand on mine as we reached our cruising attitude. "I love you Larry." I returned the smile and saying to her. "Sorry it took so long."